Copyright © 2008 by Paul Frank Industries.
All rights reserved.

Written and illustrated by Parker Jacobs.
The illustrations in this book were digitally rendered.

Library of Congress Cataloging-in-Publication Data
Paul Frank Industries, Inc.
Only in dreams : a bedtime story / a Paul Frank book.
p. cm.
Summary: Julius and his friends discover that they can
have all sorts of adventures in their dreams.
ISBN 978-0-8118-6024-6
[1. Dreams—Fiction. 2. Monkeys—Fiction. 3.
Animals—Fiction. 4. Bedtime—Fiction.] I. Title.
PZ7.F85154Onl 2008
[E]—dc22
2007016357

Manufactured in China.

10 9 8 7 6 5 4 3

Chronicle Books LLC
680 Second Street
San Francisco, California 94107

www.chroniclekids.com
www.paulfrank.com

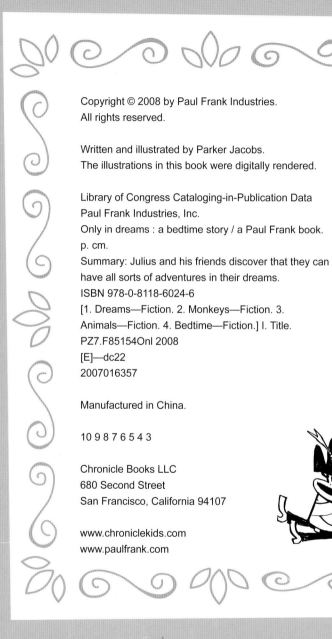

For more on Julius and Paul Frank
Industries, visit **www.paulfrank.com**.

**For Darla
& Annalena**

Only in Dreams

A BEDTIME STORY

Written & Illustrated by
Parker Jacobs

a paul frank book

chronicle books·san francisco

Hi, I'm JULIUS, and it's bedtime for me!

I love bedtime because when I sleep, I dream.

And when I dream,
I can do anything
I can imagine.

I start by closing my eyes.

It's dark at first, but then
I find a glimmer of a dream.

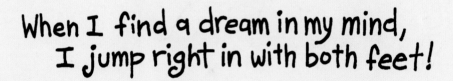

When I find a dream in my mind,
I jump right in with both feet!

Flying is just ONE thing I can
do in my dreams.
Anything is possible!

I could have
an elephant trunk...

...three heads...

...Lobster claws...

...or a potato body!

In my
dreams
I can be
SUPER
TALL.

Or I can be

Teeny Tiny.

Dreams can take me places
I've never been before,
like to a magical castle in the clouds!

Now I'm paddling down a strawberry-milk river, near a frosted-cupcake village.

If it gets too scary,
I won't worry, because I can
just dream about something else.

Now I'm a good-guy pirate
Saving a fair Lady
from bad buccaneers!

And it's the first concert
on the moon!

I ♥ U

I'm on top of the **WORLD**!

I've caught the sun!

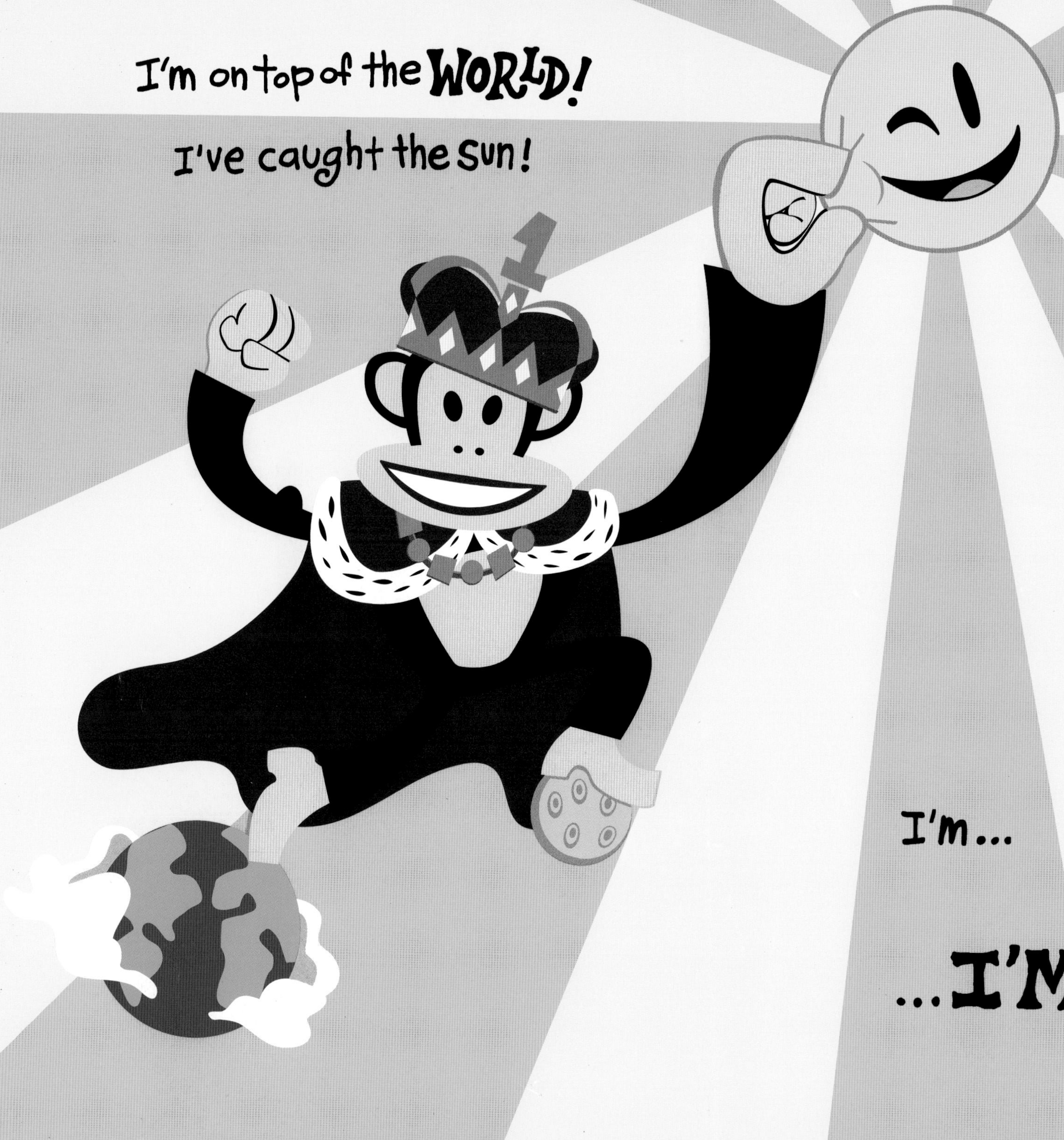

I'm...

...**I'M**...

I'm awake?

THE END
(UNTIL NEXT TIME!)